Julian Vaughan Hampton

The Contradiction

Conflicting reflections through a broken mirror

"The Contradiction" by Julian Vaughan Hampton. ISBN 1-58939-432-1.

Published 2003 by Virtualbookworm.com Publishing Inc., P.O. Box 9949, College Station, TX , 77842, US. ©2003 Julian Vaughan Hampton. All rights reserved. No part of this publication may be reproduced, stored in a retrieval system, or transmitted in any form or by any means, electronic, mechanical, recording or otherwise, without the prior written permission of Julian Vaughan Hampton.

Manufactured in the United States of America.

The Contradiction

Conflicting reflections through a broken mirror

The contradiction uses two fictional autobiographies to literarily weave the lives of childhood friends growing from adolescence to adulthood. It chronicles their physical, spiritual and emotional struggle with ethical decisions adjusted by temptation.

It tells the story of the criminal underworld plaguing a midwestern city, the desire to change the community, and the battle to change a man's soul.

Chris Parker and James Johnson are best friends growing up in the city of Milwaukee, Wisconsin. Their lives collectively evolve, despite their white and black races. What they share is a horribly painful event forever linking their lives. Every decision they make is riddled with questions and contradictions. Will they live for today, or prepare for tomorrow. Will they leave the past behind, learn from the past, or will it come back to haunt them. Through every decision one question remains; will either learn their lesson in time?

PROLOGUE

"Am I dying? I'm not sure. This pain is unbearable, unfathomable. Am I dying? I've never seen this much of my own blood before. Does this mean that I am dying?"

CHAPTER 1
CHRIS PARKER

December 20, 1977 was a day that stayed permanently embedded in my mind. It was an unseasonably warm day for Milwaukee, Wisconsin at that time of year. The persistent sun forced its warmth upon the city. Only the holiday decorations gave any indication Christmas was less than five days away. The lack of snow had no bearing on my awareness of the season.

I was an eager, blue- eyed child, anxiously waiting for Santa Claus's arrival. Every morning I asked how much longer it was until Christmas, and my father's steadying reply was, "You'll know when we stop hiding the presents from you". Like any five year old, I could hardly wait for the moment to come.

My father was a lieutenant on the police force, well respected and a believer in justice. He was a large, strong man, as dedicated to his family as he was to his job. Intense blue eyes intimidated, but his warm trademark winks made everyone feel comfortable. As for myself, my childhood trademark was a bad haircut, the recipient of untimely crew cuts. At least that day my mother saved my hickory colored locks from my father's trusty army clippers.

My father worked the streets just as vigorously as the lower ranking officers, believing 'real police work' was done outside the office. While my father was working, I spent a majority of my time down at the corner store with my best friend James Johnson. Our family had enough money for a babysitter, but my father felt more comfortable keeping an eye on me himself. The corner store was in his patrolling district.

James and I were a lot alike, naive, and loyal to each other's friendship. Being white and having a black best friend never mattered to me. The hate filled world never seemed to reach inside the innocent boundaries of our youth. Our time was filled playing kickball, or playing a game called tip-out. We spent many afternoons foolishly dancing to the disco music playing on the store radio, watching our reflections in the glass.

My father, Lieutenant Ben Parker, used a majority of his lunch breaks to check on me at the corner store and to talk to the store's manager. The manager was James's father, Royal Johnson, another genuinely good man. Royal was a tall, slight man with brown skin and a goatee.

On that day, my father again brought me down to the store to play with James. We stood outside as our father's talked and laughed inside. As usual, my father was trying to persuade Mr. Johnson to give his some free day-old doughnuts.

I saw two men in a rusted white pickup truck ride past us. At the time I thought they were lost, but later I would know differently. They drove around the store a second time and parked in front of the store.

James seemed more curious, watching the men inside of the store. I tried to get his attention, thinking only of continuing our entertainment. I heard some talking inside, then gunshots being fired. There were maybe three or four at most. My father told me how to use his police radio, so I ran his squad car and called for help.

"Help, my daddy's shooting at somebody," I cried.

They knew me down at the station, so they were sure this was no prank.

"Where are you Chris? Where's your father," asked the officer.

"At the corner store," I replied.

I was so scared that I dropped the radio and ran into the store. I found I found my father in front of the counter lying on the floor. James was on the side of the counter with his fallen father. I grabbed my daddy, screaming, crying and hoping my tears would revive him. I remember seeing the wound above his blood covered badge and hearing the pain laden gurgle of his voice.

No last words, at least ones I could recognize. No short speeches, just one final gasp and that was the end. I smelled the scent of alcohol, marijuana and piss as the first crook ran by. The second criminal stared greedily at the cash register, frantically grabbing the dollars out of it. He even took the time to pick up the change spread across the floor, and then spit on my father's body.

Even crueler was the way he treated James. He struck the small, five-year old child in the head with the butt of his gun as James lay over his father's lifeless body. Maybe he was in shock, but James did not cry. He had this cold, vengeful look in his eyes, rarely viewed in a child of his age. He stood in a state of hypnosis, grasping the crimson edge of his tee shirt.

The dusty, blonde haired criminal looked at James in disgust as he left. Help finally arrived, but only after the thugs left. When the ambulance arrived, it was too late. The chief who took the report handed my father's badge to me and rubbed my head. I felt lucky I had something. James had nothing to hold on to.

CHAPTER 1
James Johnson

It was near the end of December in 1977 when my childhood was forever taken away. I lived in one of the worst neighborhoods in Milwaukee, cradled by lawlessness and pessimism. The ringing sounds of gunfire were heard more frequently than the bells signifying the Christmas season.

The mild winter weather gave the criminals an additional period to terrorize the community.

Although I was barely five years old, I wasn't afraid of my surroundings. My city was full of division, with cultures subconsciously regulated to their destined sides of town. Within a single block, hopeless projects enviously stood across from lavish homes. It was just part of growing up in Milwaukee.

I was a shy child; at least to those I didn't know. Even at that age, my mind carried remnants of days gone by. I remembered when my parents loved me and loved each other. I remember the joy of the Christmas season. Those moments seemed like lifetimes ago. They caused me to remember how quickly drugs could destroy a family.

My daddy was a hardworking man named Royal Johnson. He truly felt he had achieved the American dream by owning his own business. The fact that he ran a twenty-four hour convenience store in the worst neighborhood in the city never troubled him. He had this strange idea that if he treated people with respect in his community, the people would respect him and his property.

My mamma wasn't set on that same dream. She was a drug addict. She always claimed to go grocery shopping, but never came back with any food. If it weren't for my grandmother, God rest her soul, mamma would have died a long time ago.

My daddy tried to get her to stop, but he too ran out of patience. The day she finally committed to a rehabilitation program, and decided to get her life together, he served her with divorce papers.

She didn't seem to care much about me, taking my sister Laena with her after the divorce. It was difficult being snatched away from Laena after spending our entire brief lives together and being suddenly placed in two different households. Although she was a year younger than me, she kept me in line and took care of me.

My mamma didn't see her as a daughter, but more as a doll to play with when she was bored and to dress pretty when it benefited her. As a child, Laena had long hair that mamma loved to braid. She had a willingness to wear anything mamma desired. A son couldn't provide her with the same benefits.

I was very young, but I still understood completely what was going on. My mamma faded out of my life after the divorce. She visited me once a week, then once a month, then never. It didn't matter to me after a while, since we weren't really that close anymore. I just didn't understand why. That was my mamma!

My daddy worked at the store a lot, so my best friend Chris and I used to play a game called 'cans' outside. We'd stay for hours attempting to bounce a ball off some aluminum cans. We couldn't afford a babysitter, so daddy came outside to check on us every once in a while. In a community filled with so much destruction, we felt safe in front of my daddy's store.

Chris's father would bring him down to the store before his shift. He was a cop, but seemed more like a second father to me. Lieutenant Parker always had a word of encouragement or advice for me. That's why 'that day' is so hard for me to accept.

Chris and I were outside playing when we saw two white men go into the store. I felt something wasn't right from the get-go. I peaked inside the store and saw my father arguing with the taller guy over something.

With a cop in the store, I thought everything would be all right. Chris's father stepped in between the two men. The shorter man pulled out a gray gun. Chris turned toward me looking puzzled.

"What's going on inside the store?"

When I turned toward him I heard a gunshot. Pop, then a pause, then pop, pop, pop. I turned and saw no one standing but the two men.

Without thought, I ran into the store. I ran past Chris's father, who was bleeding on the floor. I stopped at my daddy, lying in a pool of blood behind the counter.

The shorter man was going through the cash drawer and looked me dead in eyes. Sickness and anger filled my small body as I saw this spiteful look in that bastard's eyes. I wished I had the experience to shoot him back.

I turned to see Chris screaming over his father and focused on the crook.

The first robber ran out, saying "come on, those lil sons o bitches might remember you".

He tried to hit me in the side of my head with his gun, but I blocked it with my hand. A small cut opened along my knuckles. I covered up my head to protect myself from another strike. A drop of blood fell from my bruised fingers onto my scalp.

It seemed my mind and body was separated, because I don't recall feeling any pain.

I stayed focused on his face. Mangy blonde hair, bushy mustache, blue eyes, faded denim jean jacket, off-colored confederate flag patch, dirty nails, yellow teeth. He had liquored breath; mud stained tennis shoes and ripped holes at the knees. I recalled it from the five seconds we exchanged eye contact.

Suddenly, he turned his back and left. He ruined our lives and just left.

My daddy was gone, though the paramedics tried to provide hope.

"We'll do all we can, son."

They don't pull the sheet over your face if they're going to save you. The police captain came in to organize the crime scene. He first talked to Chris, giving him Lieutenant Parker's badge. Moments later, he came to me and caressed the top of my head.

"Stay strong, young man," he said. "We'll find the men that did this."

He had this falsely confident look on his face. Still, I nodded in affirmation to his words.

CHAPTER 2
CHRIS PARKER

After the funerals, the stench of death permeated my clothing. I rustled them off, crying and stuffing them under my bed. I spent the night laying face down in my pillow, weeping and mourning my father.

James came to stay with my mother and myself. His mother was never in his life, so my mother and I became his family. It probably wasn't the best time for my mother to take on that responsibility, especially with all of the pain she was dealing with.

She liked James, but most of the time the three of us spent together, she was silent. At times, I would creep close to her face and make sure she was still breathing. Although her vitals were functioning, her life force had been drained away.

My mother's appearance no longer mattered to her. Her soft brown hair was kept in a frizzy, elderly bun. Her housecoat corrupted any intention of fulfilling the day's agenda. Mother's days were spent blankly gazing at the television from the security of my father's chair.

Making eye contact with her caused her tremendous grief. I possessed all of my father's features, especially his eyes. It was difficult to see my mother cry, so I avoided our house as much as possible. We spent a majority of our time running the streets.

Our neighborhood was the breeding grounds for gang activity. Two main groups that battled for the territory month after month were the "Tre' Eights" and the "Lil Nation". The Tre' Eights street gang originally lay claim to the entire area. Gang members wore a fragment of green clothing with their black attire on a daily basis. More than forty-five members resided in our neighborhood, with larger numbers spread throughout the city. They were known as the 'O G's', or the original gangsters because their age ranged from twenty-five to age fifty. They focused on the business of strong-armed robbery.

The other gang was called Lil Nation. The territory they claimed began at bus station and ran east of Fondulac Avenue. They were a smaller group than the Tre' Eights, but far more dangerous and unpredictable. Young and aggressive, each one felt disrespected for no apparent reason. They used violence as a response to every discussion. The Lil Nation's weren't concerned with making money, only with claiming a territory.

The two rivals battled endlessly over a deteriorating neighborhood that any sensible person would avoid. Unfortunately, James and I weren't very sensible teens.

That area bordered the location many of the wayward youths spent their leisure time. It was where James and I could escape the pain of the past and become part of the detrimental present.

We carried ourselves like thugs, mirroring every trait that image featured. Our representations of being thugs approached exaggeration, from our "gangster limp" to our "do rags".

Committing petty crimes were daily activities for James and I. We went from stealing bicycles to stealing cars for joyrides and sold the stereos for extra money. Our ability to avoid getting caught became our biggest asset. Everyone knew what we were doing, but there was no proof to convict us of anything.

As our reputation grew throughout the neighborhood, we were dubbed with the nicknames "Quick" and "Milk". I was called Milk because I was white and they considered me "cool". James was given the name Quick, as in Nestle Quick, because we were always together.

Unfortunately, the Lil Nation's caught wind of our roguish activities in their territory. They already disliked James because he had no interest in joining their gang, but they hated me because they thought I was trying to "be black".

We heard that they were looking for us, so we monitored our steps closely. The Lil Nations found us anyway. We were returning from our hang out spot when four of the gang members approached us. Their attire gave no evidence of their identities from a distance, but as they moved closer, their tattoos indicated their gang affiliation. As they walked toward us, James nudged me with his elbow.

"Be ready, Milk," he said.

The largest guy approached me, stopping inches away from my face.

"What's up, boy," he said.

His spittle flew onto my face. I calmly wiped it away.

"Yeh, what's going on?"

"We've been looking for you, Milk."

"For what?"

"We just needed to holler at you," he said. "Let's go over here and talk."

He put his hand on my shoulder, trying to coax me away from James. I turned toward my friend and watched him having a heated discussion with the two remaining Lil Nations.

"I don't care who you say you are," James said.

I saw the smaller youth grab James's arm. When James pushed him away, I knew the time for conversation was over.

The largest guy wrapped his arm around my neck, trying to choke me, while the other grabbed my legs. They wanted to drag me into a corner to prevent James and I from fighting together. I kicked, bit and squirmed until I slipped out of their grasp. I thrust my head upward and smashed the bridge of the largest member's nose. Blood poured down his face and onto the concrete.

I noticed a black sedan driving down the street, and waved my arms to get the driver's attention. The sedan turned and sped away.

The smaller gang member chased me, holding a gun behind his back. Knowing I couldn't outrun his bullets, I ducked behind the corner of a house. I pressed myself against the siding and waited for him to run by. When he sprinted around the corner, I swung at his face as hard as I could. I mistimed my swing, but still struck him enough to knock him off his feet.

While he regained his balance, I reached for his weapon. We wrestled for possession of his gun. The black sedan slowly drove toward the altercation. I saw the sedan's window roll down, but the Lil Nation had his back to the car. A black man with a green bandanna aimed a rifle at us through the passenger window. Six shots were fired at us. In the same instance, my finger hit the trigger of my foe's gun during the struggle.

Whether it was the fatal shot from the Tre' Eight's gun, or from his own firearm, the young man dropped to the ground. The sedan raced away and I ran in the opposite direction. My shirt was spotted with blood, of which little was that of my own. I ran through a hole in a chain link fence and ran into James. His face was bruised, but he seemed to be in decent shape.

"Chris, what happened," he asked.

"Man, I have no idea what happened."

I didn't want to believe I had killed a man. A fistfight was one thing, but this was entirely different. I kept it all to myself.

We started walking away, when suddenly the police pulled up with their guns drawn. We were frisked and thrown into the back of a squad car. The last flicker of innocence was snuffed out. Even though James was next to me, I felt no comfort. To make matters worse, Captain Allen, my father's close friend, was arresting me.

He didn't look me in the eyes. I sensed he was repulsed by my involvement. After tightening the handcuffs on my wrists, he forcefully slammed the door of the squad car.

CHAPTER 2
JAMES JOHNSON

My life became extremely difficult after the burial of my daddy. My mamma wanted no part of taking responsibility for me, so I stayed with Chris and his mother Eileen. It was my only option, other than residing in a group home. I felt extremely uncomfortable living in Captain Parker's home. We weren't allowed to touch anything that had a connection to Chris's father, or bring up any memories we held of him. Our time together was filled by attempts to stay out of each other's way.

Eileen was a nervous breakdown waiting to happen. She stopped working at the bank in Brown Deer, and spent her days cooking abnormally large meals. She was a shaken woman, barely strong enough to care for her son, much less herself or myself.

Chris treated his mother with tremendous disrespect after his father died. He purposely disobeyed her, and treated her as if Captain Parker's death was her fault. He sat in his father's place at the dinner table, came in at all times of the night and refused to help Eileen around the house. I couldn't bear to see his mother deal with such hardship. I would have given anything for a mother who loved me half as much as Eileen loved Chris.

As I strayed further and further away from Chris's house, he accompanied me, as usual. We felt it was good for both of us to give Eileen some space.

From the age of twelve to age fifteen, we aggressively acted out our frustration. There were so many negative opportunities out there for us, so we reached for each one. First came the shoplifting, and later the car theft. Burglary wasn't out of the question for both of us.

School wasn't important to us, just a place to spend the day and meet girls. We were proud of the bad reputation we were making for ourselves. People either walking on the other side of the street when we came, or treated us like celebrities.

Everyone thought that we were bad kids, except my friend Denise. She was a sweet, honey-skinned girl, a flower in a concrete jungle. We had known each other since the age of five, when she would jump rope with the other girls near my daddy's store. She was the one person I didn't have to act tough around.

Her parents didn't like me, although they never took the time to get to know me. She would sneak out to the park at night to see me. We sat on the swings and talked for hours. There were no ulterior motives, and no hugging or kissing. We just talked. It was the one time we could escape the frustration of our lives. We never thought of ourselves as boyfriend and girlfriend, just as friends. Our relationship was perfect as it was, at least at that time.

Soon after my fifteenth birthday, Chris and I had the biggest of our confrontations with the two most prevalent street gangs in the city. The gangs were the "Tre' Eights" and the "Lil Nation". Both were major players in the criminal activity plaguing the city and were bitter rivals.

Living right in the area bordering their territories allowed me to stay sensibly neutral in their rivalry. The Lil Nations tried to convince me to join their gang, but I decided to just avoid them altogether. They assumed that I thought I was too good for them and grew to dislike me. They hated Chris, thinking he was a "wanna-be". It was impossible for them to understand that Chris's personality was a product of the surroundings in which he grew up.

We often hung out with a number of lost teens on the edge of Lil Nation's territory. There weren't any skirmishes with them before, so we had no reason to believe there would be another on that day.

We left our spot and were approached by four Lil Nations. Two of them walked over to talk to Chris, while the other two confronted me. I told Chris to "be ready".

"What's going on Quick," said the first Nation.

"I'm just trying to get outta here. Why, what's up?"

The second Nation came along the side of the first.

"We hear you've been moving in on our business."

The first Nation interrupted.

"You seem cool, Quick. I'd be a shame to have to crack your scull."

He pushed his open palm against the side of my head. I got annoyed with their intimidation. Out the corner of my eye I saw the other two Lil Nation's urging Chris away from me.

"I don't give a damn who you say you are, you betta not touch me again," I screamed.

I forced his hand away from my shoulder and started swinging wildly. The first Nation was much smaller, so I ran at him, throwing a barrage of punches at his face. He went down easily. It was a more difficult struggle against the larger member. While we fought, I grew concerned about Chris. He was out of my sight. It wasn't until four or five minutes of fighting that we heard gunshots. The Nation looked at me, and frantically ran away from the noises.

I proceeded toward the gunfire, hoping Chris wasn't at the wrong end of the chamber. My nose was bloody and my face hurt, but I was in fair condition. I ran into Chris walking on the other side of a fence. His shirt was stained with blood.

"Man, are you alright," I asked?

He mumbled something I could barely hear.

While walking home, the cops approached us with guns pointed in our direction.

"Freeze, or I'll blow you little ass off."

My body wanted to run, but my mind knew that was a quick way to die. I dropped to my knees and waited for them to handcuff me.

A recognizable face came near me. It was Captain Allen. I hadn't seen him since the death of my father. He told the arresting officer to leave us with him.

I felt nauseas as I entered the squad car. The police threw Chris in through the other side. We didn't even look at each other. This day was inevitable. I watched the officers shaking their heads at us, while the squad car drove away.

CHAPTER 3
CHRIS PARKER/JAMES JOHNSON

We arrived at the police station, escorted by Captain Allen. He didn't take us to the normal holding cell, but rather ushering us back to his office.

His office was reminiscent of a scrapbook, with hundreds of newspaper clippings pasted along the four corkboards. Maps with specific areas highlighted, along with numerous awards filled the remaining vacant wall space. Above Captain Allen's stout desk was a gray-rimmed clock set ahead by five timely minutes. Its movements bordered on malfunctioning, with the hour hand suddenly springing ahead, then returning to its earlier position. There were no pictures of his family on his desk, only a photo of the captain posing in front of a gun rack.

The captain pulled out two chairs from in front of his desk, pointed to them, and then pointed to us. We cautiously sat in our appointed places. Captain Allen slowly cracked each knuckle of his balled fists, breathing heavily.

He propped himself onto his old wooden desk, every bit of his 300 pounds testing its stature. Scratching the top of his balding afro, he restrained from making eye contact with us. He picked up his stainless steel mug, softly blew on the brim, and began to talk to us.

"Its hard for me to see you boys like this. I knew both of your fathers and neither one of you would have acted this way if they were alive. I know one, or both of you, were involved in the death of that boy. Is anyone willing to volunteer any information?"

The room remained silent. Captain Allen's eyes began to bulge out as he raised his voice.

"You fellas would do well to talk to me. After me, only God can save you."

He took a long, deep breath.

"So, what happened?"

Neither of the accused answered his question. The captain slammed his palm against the desk.

"Dammit, don't you see that I'm trying to help you. Do you want to spend the next twenty years in a cell? Is that what you want? I can't count the number of guys I put away. Those guys were ten times tougher than both of you. I'm sure they would love to get their hands on a wanna-be thug and the son of a cop."

He reached into his holster.

"If you're gonna kill yourself anyway, why don't I just do the job for you?"

He pointed the gun at point blank range to James, and then at Chris. Back and forth he waived the firearm, while the young men pressed to the back of their seats.

"Oh the hell with it, just shoot each other!"

He handed Chris his service revolver, while pulling his backup twenty-two-caliber gun out of his ankle holster. Both teens backed away from the guns.

"Why don't you want to do it," asked the captain?

"Because we don't want to die," said James.

The captain pointed at his head.

"Think about it. If you keep on doing what you're doing, you are going to die. No if, ands, or buts about it."

The room turned silent again.

"Look guys, I know what this neighborhood does to people. I've seen it a thousand times, but you have a chance to turn it around. If I didn't respect your fathers, I would have given up on you a long time ago. I'm the reason you're not in jail for burglary right now. Don't you still remember your father's blood like I do? Did you have to carry the casket, or console the families like I did? You should be sick to death disgracing both of your father's memories like this. I cleaned up their blood myself James. I cleaned out your father's locker, Chris. I closed their lifeless eyes to give your families peace when their bodies were seen. For their friendship I owe them a lifetime of favors, but I'll only use one of them on you."

He crouched down in front of the chairs, placing a hand on each of the boys' shoulder.

"Here's the deal. You swear to me you'll turn your lives around and I'll move the investigation away from you. We'll call it a gang related homicide by a rival gang. The Lil Nation's won't testify anyway. I haven't turned the paperwork yet. All you have to do is stay out of trouble. If word on the street gets back to me about you, I'll drag you down myself. Either way, I'll sleep fine knowing I did all that I could."

CHAPTER 3
CHRIS PARKER

Something about what he said tore into me; reviving all the pain I felt when my father was killed. Captain Allen was right. My father wouldn't have allowed me to turn out this way. No one knew that I killed a man, but as long as they didn't, I still had an opportunity to change my life and wipe the slate clean. The captain laid it all on the table, and if I didn't listen, I would surely pay the price.

I wanted to be just like my father. He had the respect, the admiration, the sense of duty, and a great purpose in his life. Everything about him was decent, the opposite of what I had become.

I told the captain that I was ready to make a change. He smiled and shook my hand. Giving me his business card, the captain pointed to the door.

"Don't let me down, son," he said.

I looked at James to see what he was going to do, and then walked out. James shook the captain's hand, and followed me out. We both cautiously left the precinct, wondering if Captain Allen would change his mind.

CHAPTER 3
JAMES JOHNSON

I had no interest in hearing the captain's lecture. Chris might have fallen for it, but I wasn't that gullible. I knew the trick, good cop, bad cop. I was just waiting for the bad cop to come into the room. He never came.

I know the captain never cared about my father. He never came over for dinner, never gave my father a birthday present, never called him at home, or anything. The cops used my daddy to get free food on their breaks. That's not what I consider friendship.

Each time he spoke, I tried to hide how irritated I was. When I looked at the wall, I saw Captain Allen's trophy case. I saw Chris's father in a picture with the captain and began to think, 'What good did the police force do for him?' It left him with a fatherless son, and a widow for a wife.

I started tuning him out, until I heard about the deal. It sounded good to me. All I had to do was apologize and leave. I was willing to do just about anything to get out of that mess. It wasn't our fault.

Chris said he was ready to make a change, so the captain let him go. I figured it would be an easy way to get out of there, so I tried the same lines as Chris. One sad look was enough for the captain to let me go free. I quickly left, realizing how easy it was to beat the system.

CHAPTER 4
CHRIS PARKER

After leaving the police station, I came to the realization that I wanted to carry on my father's legacy. Upon my graduation from high school, I set my intentions on joining the military. It was the first rung I needed to climb to reach my goal of working as a police officer.

The question concerning which line of service I would enlist still remained. The air force seemed like an adequate choice. I watched enough combat films to gain an idea about their duties. Walking proudly down the runway with my helmet tucked near my side was an appealing concept. I fell in love with the speed and power of the aircrafts. There was only one problem with the air force. My weak stomach wouldn't allow me to fall more than ten feet without feeling queasy.

Joining the marines was an interesting option. I knew it was a branch that would truly test me. The marines had a reputation that preceded itself. The positive reputation barely balanced the negative aspect the marines had long rumored. Men both lost their minds and

quit that branch, or they overcame the excruci-
ating process and became maddened. Neither
one was a choice I was willing to make.

The navy was out of the decision altogether.
My inability to swim made me ineligible for that
line of service. The plans to learn how to swim
on my sixth birthday lay at the grave of my father at the age of five.

The only valid choice was the army. The recruiter visited me time after time in high
school, attempting to convince me to enlist.
They were surprised when I finally called them
to join.

It felt like a swift process, going from the
recruiter's office to the military barber for a
haircut. After receiving my shots, I easily
passed my physical assessment test.

On our first day of basic training, we were
given our training fatigues. At that moment, I
became a number and a last name. The camp
was designed to be a humbling experience, but
I was proud to wear my first uniform, a dingy
gray tee shirt with the word 'army' written
across it. Our drill sergeant, named Sergeant
Howard, was an angry man. He looked like the
stereotypical army guy, from his crew cut and
piercing green eyes, to his horrible smelling cigar.

"My name is Sergeant Howard, and for the
next eight weeks, I'll be called Sir. Is that
clear?"

"Sir, yes sir," we shouted.

"It will be my goal to eliminate as many of
you as possible from this camp so I can go on
vacation. There's a bucket in front of my office,

so when you're ready to leave, just leave your fatigues in it. I'll take care of the paper work. Believe me, I don't mind. Maybe I'll send you a damn Christmas card or something."

"I'll be expecting you to do whatever I say, whenever I say it, with no questions asked. I expect your bunks exquisitely prepared, your asses ready for drills, and ready to work day and night for the next nine weeks. I've done this for thirty-two years, so don't any of you even think about playing any games. I'm paid to work you into ready made fighting machines."

He turned to the other sergeant.

"Damn, they sent us some real winners this time."

The sergeant walked along the lined up groups. There were all shapes and sizes of individuals with dreams to join the armed services. Unfortunately, fate had dealt them Sergeant Howard. He walked around us, looking into each of our eyes. Each person was scanned for a weakness, and when the sergeant found it, he simply smiled and spit on our shoes.

"I thought I'd help you get started shining your shoes," he said.

The other sergeant laughed along with him. I couldn't imagine one man having so much hatred, for no reason. He ran us long and exhausting distances. Half of our troop turned in their uniforms on the first day. Verbally abusive, and to those more withdrawn, physically abusive, he showed his intentions. He truly wished to eliminate all of us.

I had no fear of him, or the tactics he used to break us. In a warped sense, he was a role model to me. The powers he waved over us consumed me. I worked as hard as I could to please everyone in charge. I enjoyed everything, from the tactical march, to the confidence course. He pushed me harder and harder. I went above and beyond every duty he asked of me. I proved I could perform everything faster and better than he required.

By the time camp ended, only four of the troop had made it. Through the graduation ceremony, Sergeant Howard never shook our hands, or gave us any recognition. He only nodded once. That was enough for me, knowing that I could overcome something few had. I only wished there was someone to share my accomplishment with.

Every once and a while, I called James and my mother to make sure they were all right. My mother moved to Texas to stay with her family. She had suffered a nervous breakdown, and needed to be taken care of.

James was 'hustling for money', as they call it in our neighborhood. I'm sure he was up to no good. He couldn't understand my desire to become a police officer, but he still supported me. I promised to visit him when my goal was accomplished.

Moving on from a successful term in the armed forces, I joined the police academy. As I anticipated, my military enlistment helped me in the academy.

Being the son of a police captain, I assumed there would be an easier ride through the training. That assumption couldn't be farther from the truth. I was held to a higher standard than anyone else, and I met every obstacle head on.

I knew my father would have been proud, as I finally received my certificate as a city of Milwaukee police officer. I savored every moment, putting on my navy blue uniform, unwrapping it from it's plastic covering, removing imagined lint from the fabric, shining each button, each cufflink, spit-shining the jet black shoes, and adjusting my hat at least twenty different ways.

After gathering myself, I hesitantly walked to the mirror. I couldn't believe how much I resembled my father in the police attire, as I made my final adjustments. I was finally a police office, just like my father. In the neighborhood, we always called the police 'the man'. Now I was the man, and I relished every minute of it!

CHAPTER 4
JAMES JOHNSON

Nothing seemed serious to me, living through my teenage years. I spent more time hanging out with my friends and chasing girls, than learning in high school. I learned how to hustle and smoke weed in my street education. I became the school rough-neck, and found pride in bullying students fearful of me. There was an air of attractiveness placed on the students with the most clout.

I was a smart youth, but finding the subjects boring, I rarely paid attention to my teachers. They always reminded me of my potential, and I only needed to apply myself. It may have been true, but there was no need, since I graduated anyway. I cheated and used intimidation to work my way through school.

For a while, I dated a girl named Regina. She was a beautiful, soft spoken young lady, but only if I had money in my pockets. When the money was scarce, she was a pain in the behind. She complained about everything I did, and was quick to tell me off. Our relationship ended after I found out she was involved with the local drug dealer.

Only three people provided a connection between what I used to be, and what I was becoming; my sister Laena, my friend Chris, and my friend Denise.

The only way my sister and I stayed in touch was the fact I lived with her from time to time. Laena spent a majority of her time working, something she obviously didn't learn from our mother. She worked at a nursing home, sometimes staying there sixty to seventy hours a week. She was tired and frustrated on a daily basis. It didn't seem worth the effort to work that hard and just barely have the ability to pay the bills. Seeing her struggle caused me to avoid her as much as possible.

My friend Denise was the real bright spot in my life. Through all the girls I dealt with, she was always there for me. Denise was a small, vibrant princess with golden skin and chestnut colored hair. Being from my old neighborhood, it seemed natural for us to end up together, someday.

She tried to talk me into changing my ways, but I refused to listen, even to her. Having her there was good for me, and I would hurt anyone who affected our relationship. Making the transition from friend to girlfriend was only a matter of time. Our relationship was strong, and the only change was the titles we referred to each other by.

Chris joined the military, for some reason I couldn't understand. Allowing someone to holler at you until you crack, or running you until you pass out, was not my ideal future. I still supported him, because he was my boy, and we kept in touch. Milk was moving up through the ranks in his field, while I was becoming an entrepreneur in the drug industry.

I reunited with one of my old running mates from high school. I didn't remember his real name, only his nickname, Big Stank. We called him that because he carried an incredibly strong odor of weed with him. Everyone knew Big Stank had visited a place by the smell that lingered in his absence. I noticed he had been wearing more expensive clothing lately, and driving a nice car. Strapped for cash, I asked him if he knew where I could find some work.

"Legal, or illegal," he asked.

"It don't even matter, man," I replied.

He was the first person to introduce me to the drug game. To see how I could handle myself, I was set up with some marijuana dime bags to sell on the street corner. It was simple; just wait on the corner and the smokers found me.

The police weren't a problem. They weren't concerned about a small time drug dealer, in an area filled with minorities. As I improved my craft, he got me a position running crack cocaine from the gas station. I stuffed the drugs in packs of gum, and the dope fiends would ask for Wrigley's, a code name for crack.

I made enough money to take care of myself and buy a little car, but I wanted more. The world owed me more. Selling crack in the inner city wasn't where the big money was. The drugs didn't come from the hood, and the people making the largest profit from it didn't live in the hood. They lived in the suburbs, where the high priced cocaine was located and used.

The stressed out white-collar businessmen, the soccer moms with rebellious kids, and the disobedient spoiled teens getting high with their friends were users, just like the crack heads.

I delivered the cocaine packages in a tow truck, using a delicate procedure to pack the cocaine between the cells in car batteries. I knew the police dogs couldn't smell it there.

At the time, I was working for Tony Lasado, a kingpin who was both charismatic and poisonous. Tony would protect an enemy if he could make money from it, or kill his own father if he shorted him on his money. He supplied me with the customer's addresses, and I delivered the drugs to them, only after the location was checked.

Success in the drug game was measured in dollars and cents. I made Tony a lot of money, therefore I was considered a successful runner. I became an important commodity to him, someone who could perform the job without using the product, or trying to start my own business. I considered myself a businessman, making more money than I could spend. I often stood in the mirror, dancing and admiring myself in my Italian silk suits, diamond earrings, and snake skin boots. I had it going on.

CHAPTER 5
CHRIS PARKER

As a member of the police force, my employment began without too much trouble. I built my credentials 'learning' from my partner, Officer Frank Adams. I didn't respect him, calling him 'Adams' and showing him the utmost disrespect. He was my senior, but since we were both beat cops, I had no reason to look up to him. He tried to give me advice, but I already knew what was going on. In the back of my mind, I was just biding time. I knew the opportunity to carry on my father's tradition was just a matter of time.

It wasn't long before I was promoted, and earned the ability to work by myself. It was time to let the city know all about Chris Parker.

My first attempted arrest was made on a domestic violence case. I was riding in my patrol car and received a call from our dispatcher. A domestic violence incident had been reported. A middle-aged woman called 911 after her husband abused her. When I arrived at the scene, I saw the man flinging his wife on to the front lawn. I rushed toward the suspect, threw him down on the asphalt, and handcuffed him.

As I forced him into the squad car, his wife pleaded for me to let him go. I told her that I couldn't because she had bruises on her face. She continued to verbally belittle me with each statement, until I drove away with her husband.

I assumed it would be an open and shut case, but I was wrong. I forgot to read him his Miranda rights, due to the woman's constant interrupted. The marks I saw on face were just dirt from the lawn. I was angered to find her face carried no bruises, although her upper torso probably did.

It didn't matter, since his wife refused to press charges. He was off scott free, and filed a police abuse charge against me. Luckily, the judge threw out the case, sighting the lack of evidence to prove the abuse. I still ended up with two weeks of desk duty.

Another problem occurred at a local high school. I was assigned to patrol a varsity basketball game. I saw a large skirmish on the top section of the bleachers. It appeared that four or five youths were beating on another young man buried beneath the pile. I followed the security guards into the altercation. Upon seeing the authorities, the kids all dispersed. The guards chased two young men down the left corridor, while I followed one youth down the right hallway. I tackled him, and decided to teach him a lesson by roughing him up. I put my weight on top of his face, pressuring it into the cold marble floor. Awkwardly twisting his arm behind his back, I shouted, "You little punks are gonna learn to leave folks alone."

The kid whimpered, "They were the ones hitting me."

I turned him over to look at his face. His lip was bloody, and his skin had large bruises.

"Dammit," I said.

He was the victim, and I let the two other aggressors get away.

One of the next criminals I apprehended was a robbery suspect. A local store had a history of robberies. There were six in all, and the same individual performed each one.

I caught the man hiding in the dumpster in the alley. The money was still stuffed underneath his shirt. I asked the storeowner if this was indeed the thief.

"Yes, that's him", he said.

Upon catching a glare from the crook, he changed his story. Intimidated, he said I had caught the wrong man. I asked for the surveillance video, and he said the camera was malfunctioning. Being the son of a crime victim, I knew that he was scared, and with good reason. I don't think he knew the repercussions of his inactions. He would surely be robbed again.

My overzealous ego had made me the laughingstock of the district. Instead of getting the same respect my father received, I was an embarrassment to his name. The terminology, 'a parker', became another word for a stupid mistake throughout my district. I vowed to find a way to change that definition.

I was assigned to an investigation of some drug spots. My career survived solely through the name of my father, so I knew that any more mistakes wouldn't be tolerated. It wasn't within the scope of my job, but I acted on a tip from an old connection. I was informed of a connection between a known drug runner and a suspected drug head man Raymone Thomas.

Raymone was a prime enemy of the drug kingpin Tony Lasado. Raymone was sneaky, maniacal, untrusting, and corrupt. He had very good fronts to cover his main business. He operating a fine eatery, a tailoring shop, and a pool hall located on the eastside.

My connection informed me of the drug runner's bad habit of using the same backpack to transport the money and the drugs to the restaurant. The pool hall had its lights on, even though the closed sign was on the door. When I saw the runner bringing the backpack to the to the pool hall, I knew something was going on. I didn't call for a backup squad, because I wanted to do it myself. My ego wouldn't let me call for backup.

When I entered the hall with my badge and gun drawn, I saw the unsuspecting drug runner with the open backpack and cocaine exposed on the pool table. I estimated there to be about two kilograms of cocaine on the table.

Confidently, I yelled, "Police, on your back".

While searching the runner for weapons, Raymone came from the back room. I pointed my gun at him, assuming someone else could be in the pool hall. My adrenaline was flowing, and I could picture my name in the paper, already.

Raymone began talking to me, seeming to already know my identity.

"Chis Parker finally caught somebody," he said.

"How do you know my name?"

He smiled.

"I know all the cops in this city."

Raymone sat on the pool table.

"I hear you've been having a little trouble on the job."

"Nah, no trouble at all," I said.

"That's not what the grapevine says. I hear you're just a joke on the force. Imagine that, the son of Ben Parker turned into a bumbling idiot."

I grew angry.

"I must not be too much of a bumbling idiot. I busted your fat ass."

Raymone's expression quickly changed.

"You did what?"

I decided to change my tone.

"You didn't do anything, Parker. How do you get the idea that you caught me, if I'm the one who decides if you leave here alive or not."

Raymone pulled out a long, Cuban cigar and lit the end.

"How did you know my father?"

"Your father and I did some work together. He scratched my back, and I scratched his. You don't make it in this world without connections."

"Look, Raymone, you're gonna have to come with me."

Raymone began to laugh.

"I ain't going nowhere with you, and you better start addressing me as Mr. Thomas."

I heard mumbling voices from behind the wall. Raymone wasn't in the restaurant alone. I slowly put my firearm away. It made no sense to pretend that I was going to use it. If Raymone decided to call for help, I was done.

"I like your attitude, Parker. It takes some kind of fool to come into my pool hall and try to arrest me. I'm gonna do you a favor."

"A favor?"

"Well, more like a deal."

I started laughing.

"I don't do deals."

"Well, then you don't do breathin."

I got the message, loud and clear.

"What is the deal, Mr. Thomas?"

"That's more like it, son. Have a seat."

I sat on the small stool near the corner of the bar.

Raymone began to speak.

"I'm a fair man, so I'll give you two choices. I want to make you successful."

"Why would you help me," I asked.

"Well, actually, we'd be helping each other. Here's how it will work. I'll provide you with the crime, the suspects, the tips, and the evidence. All you have to bring is the handcuffs."

"That's it?"

"That's it," he replied.

"And what's in it for you?"

"Peace of mind. You keep the police out of my business and my enemies out of my hair."

"And what if I don't? What's my other choice?"

Raymone shook his head.

"It's simple. I'll file you away with the other guys who wouldn't cooperate."

Raymone slowly walked around the pool tables, stroking each one he passed.

"I got a place where I keep people like that, or at least those I like."

He knocked on the pool table.

"Ain't that right, Bobby?"

I heard an eerie mumbling from inside the pool table.

"What the hell is wrong with you? You can't put somebody inside a pool table and expect them to live."

Raymone giggled.

"Who said I wanted him to live?"

He grabbed a pool stick and a chalk square.

"Calm down, Parker. Bobby and I are in the middle of negotiating a deal. Right Bobby?"

He knocked on the table. The mumbling inside the pool table ceased.

"Don't worry. He's only been in there a couple of days. If he weren't my brother in law, I might not have been so patient. I got a feeling that he'll come around, though."

"Man, you're sick."

"You ain't seen sick, yet. I suggest you take my offer."

I quickly weighed my options. Raymone's threats didn't bother me much. I didn't care about dying, because I barely had a life. I stopped caring about doing the right thing some time ago. A cold heart was the worst affliction a cop could have. I no longer cared about justice. I just wanted the prestige, the admiration, and the entitlements that went along with the successful arrests. I hoped agreeing with Raymone would bring about the desired results.

"All right, Mr. Thomas, lets do it."

"That's what I like to hear. I'll have someone call you with your instructions."

He walked toward me with his large, spotted hand extended.

"Nice doing business with you," he said.

He shook my hand with a vice like grip, looking through my eyes.

"Yeh, you too."

He placed ten one hundred dollar bills into my palm, and patted me on the back. Tucking the cash into my pocket, I left the pool hall. The rumbling inside the pool table was followed by faint cries for help. I shook my head and left. There was nothing I could do.

CHAPTER 5
JAMES JOHNSON

With large amounts of money came large amounts of attention, both positive and negative. I was trying to keep the negative exposure at a minimum. I gave everyone the impression that I was working overtime towing and repairing cars.

No one knew of my illegal activities, not even Denise. I fooled her into thinking I was making an honest dollar. She was proud of me and urged me to continue my hard work. Even Denise was impressed with the money I was bringing in. She enjoyed being spoiled. We often celebrated my financial upcoming recreationally, as well as intimately. I figured she didn't know the truth about how I made my money, as long as the money continued to come in.

One night, I was at the shop setting up some car batteries for the next shipment. I often performed the service ahead of time because it was a delicate procedure. The drugs were placed between the battery cells. I rigged them so if they were opened wrong, they would explode, and the acid would destroy the cocaine.

I worked under one dim light that was strung across an overhead beam. All the other lights were kept off to avoid calling any attention to my work. There were three sharp knocks on the service door. I peered from behind the hood of the truck, but no one could be seen through the dirty glass.

The doorknob turned back and forth, and finally clicked. Slowly, the door opened. I searched myself for the twenty-five caliber gun I always kept near me, but my jacket was on the other side of the garage.

A voice called, "Hello, anybody here?"

"Sorry buddy, the shop's closed."

Looking around the truck, I saw a small Italian man draped in a black leather coat. With dancing eyes, he surveyed the garage. He walked over to the side of the truck.

"The name's James, right?"

"Yeh, but I told you the shop was closed."

He extended his hand toward me.

"Calm down. Tony sent to talk to you. He's got a new job for you."

"Man, I don't know what you're talking about."

Just the mention of Tony's name caused me to start sweating.

"You know damn well what I'm talking about. Tony wants to move you inside the or ganization, and I'm supposed to take your place here."

I wiped my face.

"Man, I'm just a mechanic. I don't even know Tony."

The man walked around the garage, touching my equipment.

"So, how do you do it?"

"Do what?"

"How do you move the stuff? I'm supposed to learn from you."

"I can't help you. You should probably leave."

"Look, if you got beef, it ain't with me. Go talk to Tony."

I knew something was wrong. No one knew about my association with Tony, and this stranger mentioned his name twice. Everyone that knew Tony understood it was suicide to casually throw around his name.

Someone had dropped the dime on me. I was sure of it. I didn't know if I had finished loading any of the batteries with cocaine. I knew I needed to get out of there. The man touched one of my wrenches and placed his finger on the tip of his tongue. I nervously searched for an escape.

When his back was turned, I jumped into a tow truck, driving away without even closing the truck's hood. Through barrels, cans, auto parts, and who knows what else, I drove. Unable to see where I was going, I found myself speeding out of the garage. To my surprise, hordes of police cars were outside the shop. Someone had sold me out. I was sure of it.

All I could think about was how disappointed Denise would be when she found out. I thought I'd be out of the drug game before I ever got caught, but this was too soon. Five or six cops dragged me out of the truck, punching me and wrestling me to the ground. I felt it would be all right, since there wasn't much evidence available in the garage.

Once again, I was thrown in a police car. I remembered that view, that stuffy odor, and those cold leather seats. It was just like old times, I guessed.

CHAPTER 6
CHRIS PARKER

My first instructions from Raymone were to wait outside an electronics store. The owner was a former drug pusher for him. He figured he could increase his profit by going into business for himself. Being the brother of one of Raymone's restaurant associates, he couldn't kill the storeowner.

I was told to arrest him at ten o'clock, the time he would be carrying a large amount of crack cocaine and money. The owner was foolish enough to believe he could schedule his drug business to coincide with his store hours. Raymone knew this, and the setup was well organized.

As the owner locked the door, I pulled up along the curb with my lights on and arrested the owner. Looking confused, he didn't try to resist my arrest. The street value of the bust was forty thousand dollars, and my chief rewarded me with an award for my stellar police work.

The next setup was planned around an alderman who tried to organize an anti-drug commission in Raymone's most prolific drug area. Raymone used one of his underlings as a fake bartender in a bar called 'The Nest'. The alderman often had a drink after his work hours. This time, when he ordered his usual, cola mixed with brand, the bartender sprinkled cocaine in his glass. Finishing his drink, the alderman left the bar and entered his brown BMW.

As he left the driveway, a blue suburban followed him, bumper to bumper. It was being driven by some of Raymone's men, but he had no idea who was driving behind him. He made several turns, driving in many different directions to evade them, but they stayed on his tail.

Frightened, he sped through red lights and stop signs, as the men following him finally pulled away.

At that time, I moved in, pulling him over on the side of the road.

"Did you see those hoodlums chasing me, officer," he asked?

"Sir, could you please step out of the vehicle," I responded.

I could see his glossy eyes, and smelled enough alcohol on his breath to justify a breath test and search his car.

"Sir, you were speeding, and you ran some red lights. Are you under the influence of any substances?"

"Of course not," he adamantly replied. "Search the car if you don't believe me. I'll take a test or whatever. I don't care."

After handcuffing the alderman, I searched his car. In the back seat were small packages of cocaine, which I threw on the trunk of his car. I could see the surprised look on his face, as he sat in shock. Claiming it wasn't his drugs, the alderman got upset.

"Somebody planted this on me, I swear it," he screamed.

I drowned out his pitiful cries by reading him his rights. I put him in the back seat of the squad car, telling him that he was going downtown for a drug test.

When his system was found containing traces of cocaine and alcohol, he was charged with possession and use of an illegal substance, disorderly conduct, traffic violations, and evading the police. His career was finished, as was the anti-drug commission.

I didn't care what happened to the alderman, as long as my career was prospering. At the police station, I attributed my arrests to my 'good ole fashion police sense'. The higher ups were starting to notice me.

For my third arrest, I needed to change the game plan I had used before. Raymone's major competitor, Tony Lasado, had a big money drug runner, but no one knew his schedule, or how he transported the cocaine supply. Raymone had him followed for a week, and knew the best way to bust him was at his place of employment. The runner worked at a repair shop on Center Street.

I couldn't be the first one to arrive again. It would cause too much suspicion. I gave the captain the information Raymone gave me. The captain, recently impressed with my improvement, decided to send an undercover officer to investigate the runner's job. All I had to do was sit back and wait for the bust to go through.

While waiting for a call to inform me of the outcome, I diligently organized my paperwork. My captain called me into his office to give me a report on my tip. He stated, "The bust was semi-successful. We caught the drug runner with some traces of cocaine at his repair shop, but not in any large quantities. Also, we had an officer seriously injured, getting struck by a car when the perpetrator tried to escape. Still, we got one criminal off the street for a while, and it was all because of your tip. Good job Parker."

I carried the momentum of that praise to my regular police work, on the beat, and throughout my paperwork. It got to a point where I made twelve to fifteen arrests per week, each one backed by overwhelming evidence. Raymone's assistance was present in every case. For two years I proved myself to the department, racking up numbers that made other districts jealous.

After passing my examination, I was pleased to receive notification of my promotion to the position of detective. I was honored, but my ego kept me from being humbled. My career was evolving, but it wasn't enough. I wanted more. I eagerly waited for Raymone's call for my next big arrest.

CHAPTER 6
JAMES JOHNSON

The police put me in a holding cell, leaving me to wonder if anyone would bail me out. I couldn't reach any of Tony's people, so I called Denise. Like a child honestly professing their mistake, I was hesitant to call her and tell her what I'd done. Disappointing her was something I tried to avoid, but I knew it was inevitable.

I slowly dialed the number, doubting my judgment with every button I pressed. I nearly hung up when she answered, but decided to take my medicine.

"Hey baby, it's James."

"James, where are you? I've been calling the shop all night. Are you alright?"

I replied, "Yeh, I'm alright. I had a little altercation with the police, and I got arrested."

"What kind of altercation?"

"I got arrested because they thought I had drugs on me. They said I ran some dude over with the truck."

"Well did you?" she asked.

Although denial would have been more beneficial to the both of us, my heart wouldn't allow me to lie to Denise. I took a deep breath, and continued our conversation.

"Yeh, I did it. I did it for us, baby. I had to provide for us and ain't no way I was gonna work at Burger King."

I could hear her voice cracking.

"How could you be so selfish? You didn't do that for us, you did it for you. I'd respect you ten times more if you worked at a fast food joint. At least I'd know you'd be there for us."

I knew Denise, and I could tell that there was something deeper that was bothering her.

"What's the real problem? I've always been there for you."

"I know, but I want you to be there for our child."

I almost fell out of my seat.

"Our what?"

Denise spoke softly, "I'm pregnant".

A rush came through my body like I had never experienced before. It was a feeling of joy, regret, and fear. The fear wasn't for what would happen to me, it was for a child whom I feared would grow up without a father as I did most of my life.

I felt regret, knowing what I did would affect all three of us terribly. My joy came from the knowledge of a part of me living inside Denise. She had been hiding her pregnancy for about four months, already. That wasn't important to me at the time. She was afraid I wouldn't want a child, knowing how I loved to run the streets. She felt that I was afraid of commitment, but she was wrong.

I asked Denise to call Chris on a three-way phone line. Maybe he could get me a better attorney than the city would provide for my trial. I heard he was doing well in the police department, so I thought he could pull some strings.

I listened to Denise initiate the conversation with Chris. From the sound of the discussion, Chris wasn't very helpful.

"I don't know why you won't help him," she said. "He's on the phone, so you can tell him yourself."

Chris and I talked for a short amount of time. He sounded concerned, yet disturbed by my call. I told him only what I wanted him to know. He was a cop now, and probably wouldn't understand the issue I was facing from my point of view.

"I can't really do anything to help you, Quick," said Chris. "The attorneys provided by the city are very good. If you're really innocent, you should be fine."

His demeanor was antagonizing. I sarcastically thanked my so-called best friend and hung up on him. I told Denise that I would be in touch with her.

I received a court appointed lawyer, one who didn't care whether I was set free or not. He was all about his paycheck. His name was Mr. Kyle, never giving me his first name because he didn't think I had reason to know him personally. I thought I was different than the other defendants, but Mr. Kyle proved I was just like any other thug.

When my trial started, I knew something was inexplicably wrong. There were far more police officers than would be expected for a trial of this nature. The bailiff announced the case.

"Case number two, three, zero, three, city of Milwaukee versus James Johnson. Judge William Doski presiding."

The judge read the charge, "The defendant is being tried for drug possession, evading arrest, resisting arrest, and attempted vehicular homicide."

'Attempted vehicular homicide?' I asked myself. Where the hell did that come from? I didn't try to run anyone over, so I had no understanding of why I was being tried for that. I received no information from Mr. Kyle. His only instructions to me were to keep quiet and stay out of the way. He announced my plea as not guilty.

There were many times I wanted to address the discrepancies, or clarify facts to help make my case, but my arrogant, misinformed, unprepared lawyer wouldn't listen. He dressed like the long lost white member of the temptation, and he slicked his hair back, combing the excess grease through it between arguments. His appearance seemed to irritate the judge, and he was scolded throughout the trial for inappropriate attire.

Poor witness selection and meaningless cross-examination points were evident in his defense. His attempt to portray the wheelchair bound undercover officer, who I supposedly ran over, as a maniacal, con artist cop, further tarnished my lawyer's credibility.

Even sitting on the opposite side of the trial, I felt the officer was a genuinely good

man. His testimony included his love for his
job, his willingness to accept the opportunity to
keep the community crime free, and what it
cost him. He spoke of the fact of never again
being able to run with his children. He was
paralyzed from the waist down.

Mr. Kyle attacked his image, even question-
ing his paralysis; I was as repulsed as the ju-
rors were. They cried when they listened to the
officer speak, but looked upon me with disdain.

A woman I didn't recognize testified against
me. She spoke of instances where I brought cocaine to her husband, and how it destroyed
their lives. Her husband took his own life in an
overdose. The prosecution's intentions were obvious. They wanted to portray me in the worst
possible light.

The one problem they faced was a lack of
physical evidence. There were traces of cocaine
on some hand tools, but what they found
wasn't enough to impact the case. An inept, using or misusing large words, and interrupting
everyone in the courtroom were back breakers
in my in my trial.

I was found guilty of possession of a con-
trolled substance and evading arrest. Luckily,
the jury felt there was no intention on striking
the undercover cop, since I didn't know that I
hit him. My sentence was three years in prison.

I was informed I could get it reduced to one
year if I turned Tony in. The idea sounded
tempting, but there was no way I could turn in
Tony. He helped me too much, plus I wouldn't
finish my sentence in prison. I'd be dead within

a week. Tony would surely find out. I decided to serve my time without snitching.

After the verdict, my lawyer didn't want to talk to me. He chose to joke around with the prosecutors rather than comfort me. As I was escorted out of the courtroom by armed guards, my lawyer bantered about which bar they all would attend that night.

CHAPTER 7
CHRIS PARKER

One afternoon, I received a call from James that disturbed me. He needed help after getting in trouble with the law. Tired of hearing James speak about his legal problems, I brushed him off. It was hard to understand why he put himself in these situations, and then looked to me for help to get out of them.

James needed a lawyer, and that wasn't something I could help him with. Besides, I wasn't about to risk the good thing I had going on by carrying him, friend or no friend. I had no idea if he committed a crime or not, but I doubted he would tell me the truth anyway. That wasn't important.

I no longer cared what he did, or what happened to him. I was a better person than he was, and he should have shown me more respect when he called me. Maybe a little jail time would remodel him into a law-abiding citizen.

After a short time lecturing James on the values of our judicial system, I received a call from Raymone.

"I got a new job for you, a real winner," he said. "I want Tony Lasado out of the picture."

There was no way I wanted to get involved with Tony, so I declined. Raymone pointed out a more appealing picture.

"Taking down one of the biggest crime bosses would make your career skyrocket. Hasn't everything else been easy? If we work together, there would be benefits for the both of us. I'd have total control of the drug industry, and you'd have all the acclamations from the police force. It's a match made in heaven. We're a team, you and me. Just remember, I made you and I can damn sure break you."

I thought about it for sometime, deciding to go along with Raymone's plan once more. The ethics I paraded out in front of the everyday citizens were far different than my actions showed behind the scenes. Total control seemed more in reach than ever.

Already, I was admired by the police department and feared by the local thugs who caught wind of my reputation. They were unaware of my farce.

The problem with bringing down Tony Lasado was the fact that everyone knew what he did, had an idea of how he did it, but no one had enough guts to stand up to him. I wondered why Raymone, with all of his tough talk and emperor like promises, seemed so hesitant to take matters into his own hands. He was akin to a wolf, bravely attacking when in a pack, yet a coward when hunting alone.

An agreement was reached between us; still his visible weakness annoyed me. I was aware of a potential double cross. Raymone would have no use for me if I took Tony down, especially with all the information I possessed about him. I needed to find a way to trap both Tony and Raymone.

How much acclaim would I receive by bringing down the two largest drug cartels in the state? How much power would I receive? How many awards would I collect? How much would my career improve? Raymone told me he would call me within the week with his plan. Hopefully, that would be enough time to create a plan of my own.

CHAPTER 7
JAMES JOHNSON

I was sent to Waupun Correctional Institution to serve my three-year sentence. Juvenile detention centers and the Milwaukee County Jail seemed like a cakewalk compared to this place.

There was concrete as far as the eyes could see, razor wire fences that soared thirty feet high, men herded like cattle to and from every location, and guards constantly focused on us, fingers glued to their triggers in anxious anticipation of our disobedience. From my first night, there seemed to be a different reaction to me than to most of the other new inmates.

The first trouble I encountered was a Latino inmate that tried to test me. At the time we were supposed to be cleaning the bathrooms, he approached me, demanding half of my meal rations for his crew's protection. When I refused, I noticed his partner coming on the side of me. I kicked the Latino inmate in the kneecap, and punched him in the throat. As he struggled to regain his breath, the guards took him away.

The guards left me alone, and his partner scurried into the crowd. The next time I saw the Latino man, he looked horrible. He was missing an eye, he couldn't talk, and his face was badly bruised. I found out later Tony was responsible for it.

In prison, Tony was a guardian angel, in a sort of diabolical way. Someone who was watching me for Tony informed him of the Latino's attempt to jack me, and he paid for it with his eye and the tip of his tongue. No one was to touch me while I was in Waupun, and I used that to my advantage.

I got all the cigarettes I wanted, and all the respect I needed to survive over the three years I was incarcerated. All of Tony's favorites were taken care of if they served time. Tony vowed to get the person who set me up, and I knew that he would. The person who did it committed the worst crime anyone could do against Tony. They messed with his money. He said he would take care of my family.

The pages of the calendar in my cell rapidly turned as my release date grew closer. I rarely heard from Denise until she finally visited me as I served my third year. Her scornful glare made it hard to even look her in the eyes. I placed my fingertips against the cloudy glass barrier. She sat far away from the glass with her legs tightly crossed.

"Girl, you don't know how much I've missed you," I said. "I can't wait to get out of here and show you how I feel."

My cute grin had no impact on Denise's demeanor. She was just as upset as she was upon her arrival.

"Look James, I'm not here to listen to your tired ass prison game. The only reason I'm here is for Theresa."

I wiped the grin from my face.

"How is my little princess?"

She moved further from the glass.

"Your little princess? You've never even seen her, and you want to call her your little princess?"

I looked around to see if anyone was listening.

"Look, I can't help what the system did to me. It's not like I didn't want to see her."

Denise moved her chair closer to the glass.

"It isn't the system, James. It's you. You made these stupid decisions and screwed up three lives.

She continually pointed her finger at the glass.

"You need to clean up your life. Don't do it for me, or for yourself, but for her."

Denise pulled out a picture of the most adorable little face I'd ever seen. It was my daughter Theresa. She was so precious, and so unaware of the failure I had become. I could see my own features in her gentle face. My head fell humbly on to the counter.

"I'm sorry baby," I said. "Does she know who I am at all?"

"Yes James, she knows who you are. I love her too much to talk bad about you. I love you too much to give up on our family."

I cried like never before, holding my face in my hand to hide the tears. I had spent so many months away that I'd already missed her first words and her first steps.

She held the picture up to the glass with one hand, and a crumpled sheet of paper in the other hand. The paper contained a scripture from the bible. It was James chapter one verse twelve. 'Blessed is the man who endureth temptation, for when he has been approved, he will receive the crown of life which The Lord has promised to those who love him.'
She called the guard over, instructing him to give me the picture and the scripture.

"We love you, James. Never forget that."

"I love you too," I replied.

Denise came to her feet.

"One more thing, James," she added. "Don't have that Tony guy come around me or our child to check up on us. We don't need his dirty money. You need to tell him to leave your sister Laena alone, too."

As she left, I wondered what she meant about my sister. Through my connections, I found out Laena was working for Tony. She apparently grew sick of hard work and a lack of money, and chose the life I had led instead. I sent a message to Tony stating I didn't want my sister involved in that business. He sent a reply informing me that she would be let out of the organization.

Spending time warming my heart with the picture of my child, and memorizing the bible passage Denise left with me, I knew that I was changing. I no longer felt like mingling with the criminals in the prison.

CHAPTER 8
CHRIS PARKER

The relationship I created with the media was built out of necessity. I needed them to write and report positive information about me, knowing full well they could either cast me in a hero's light, or create a shadow of doubt over every action I performed. I felt I had moved passed the point where people double-checked my work. It was important to keep it that way.

Every interview the media requested was conducted. I gave them all the answers they looked for and my responses were all given with charisma. I knew each reporter's first and last name, and issued statements when the chief was handling other business.

My appeal to the media was rewarded with glowing journalism, while my intentions and integrity were never questioned. It also worked perfectly for the media, as they had full access to information other officers wouldn't give them.

One news and talk radio host didn't follow status quo, and was critical of everything the police department and I did. Her name was

Jacquelyn Reynolds, host of Community Justice; a talk show on am 940. I had heard rumors about the way she would shred police departments and public officials. Listening to the program for myself, I found the rumors to be true. She named people's names, especially mine, and raised issues about my convenient appearances at successful drug busts. She questioned my lack of appearances at community events. They called her 'the shark' and I could see why.

I needed to find out who she was, and possibly alter her opinion of me. She had the chance to be a major impediment to me, or a catalyst in my ongoing success if I could change her mind. I heard she would be at the mayor's banquet. That would be a perfect opportunity to meet and persuade her.

At the mayor's banquet, I scanned the room, intensely trying to figure out what this nosy busybody looked like. I found her nameplate at a table, so I sat conveniently at the next table.

I waited to see the woman who, by the minute, was filling me with a slow burning hatred. Instead, I saw a jewel. A gorgeous woman with lock brown hair, captivating almond colored eyes, a sexy business suit, a confident, professional demeanor, and the most luscious legs I'd ever seen.

'That couldn't be her', I thought to myself.

I had built up so much disdain for her, but seeing her, I stood in awe.

I introduced myself to her.

"Hello, Mr. Reynolds, I'm Detective Chris Parker."

"It's Ms. Reynolds, and I know who you are," she sternly said.

I replied, "I just wanted to tell you how much I appreciate the work you do for the community."

She rolled her eyes at me.

"Thank you, but your flattery will not affect my show, or its contents. If you spent more time serving the community, and less time selfishly serving yourself, you could make a difference."

Avoiding the fact I was offended, I slithered back into my chair. I wished her a good night before I left the event. I knew I would see her again, and that would be the time to change her opinion of me. The three people stopping me from all the fame, respect, and power this city could offer were Tony, Raymone, and Jacquelyn. Each of them would have to be dealt with.

CHAPTER 8
JAMES JOHNSON

While things were getting harder in prison, I was finding inner peace within me. The prisoners I had aligned with drew back from me, as my personality began to change. I became more spiritual, and spent most of my time with another inmate they called Preach. Time was good to Preach, giving him the face of a thirty year old, though he was midway through his fifties. He looked like a Muslim, but the similarities stopped there. Most of the guards and inmates thought he was insane, talking in tongues and speaking scriptures loudly in response to their vulgar comments.

I thought he was crazy myself, until he confronted me at our exercise period.

"God bless you young man," he said.

I merely nodded in response.

"Did you know that there was something special about you?"

I hunched my shoulders.

"I don't know why the Lord sent me specifically to you, but he wants to bless you."

I replied, "I'm sure there's people who deserve to be blessed more than me. Why don't you tell your 'god' to see them?"

Preach stroked his long steely beard.

"I serve one God, The Lord, The Almighty, The maker of heaven and earth. If he instructed me to speak to those 'more worthy', as you say, then I would obey. His instructions were for me to speak to you."

I looked around at the other inmates. Most focused their attention on their own activities, except two smaller residents. They whispered and pointed toward our area.

"What the hell are you looking at," I barked.

Their eyes moved toward a different direction.

"I thought so."

Preach shook his head.

"All that aggression, all that intensity, all that fire. I believe that's what He wants."

"Man, I don't know what you want from me, but I got to go."

Preach put his hand on my shoulder.

"It's not what I want from you; it's what He wants from you. If you used that zeal within you to win some souls...My son, do you know The Lord, Jesus Christ?"

"I used to know him, until he let the people closest to me die horribly and painfully. What kind of god would allow his servants to die that way, but let their murderers live?"

He responded, "The same God that sacrificed his only son for our salvation. Everything has a plan and a purpose, son. Life and death all have their purposes, but with Christ there is life and life more abundantly."

Although my appearance showed my lack of interest in Peach's statements, my heart heard every word he said. I began my attempt to reestablish my relationship with God. I was already reading the scripture Denise gave me many times a day. Preach showed me how to interpret the bible, and in return I kept the rougher inmates off his back.

I only had a small amount of time left to serve. In my mind were visions of times spent singing melodic lullabies to my daughter.

I spotted the person I least expected, yet most wanted to see, at the lunch table. He always ate with his head down, so I never recognized him before. I remembered that mangy hair, those bloodshot eyes, and that stench. It was my father's killer. How ironic, the idea we would end up in the same prison. He was the beginning of my road to this godforsaken place, and a key to the failure I had become.

He sat there, not even knowing whose life he affected, and not caring. He mocked me with an idiotic expression fixed onto his face. With so many years passing, this demon's appearance hadn't changed one bit. Thousands of emotions swirled through my soul as I watched this man. It was as if I were in a horror movie, hearing a voice shouting 'kill, kill, kill'. Preach was sitting next to me, observing me staring at this man and tightly clutching a homemade shank in my right hand.

He asked, "What's wrong, James?"

"That's the man who killed my father. He's got to die."

Preach grabbed my wrist with a vice like grip.

"Thou shall not kill. Thou shall not kill. Thou shall not kill."

His voice grew from a whimper to a yell. He repeated himself several more times, asking me to reach into my sock. I did as he asked, realizing that was the place where I kept my daughter's photo. As I held the picture, I instantly spoke along with him.

"Thou shall not kill."

With a sudden change in my heart, I walked past the killer, touching him on the shoulder.

"I forgive you," I whispered in a tearful voice. The man looked confused, not knowing who I was or what I meant. It was one of the hardest things I'd ever done in my life. I'd much rather shove the shank through his chest, but this was the right thing to do. Once again, I could see that I was growing.

I was finally able to talk the courts into supplying me with a new lawyer. He convinced the judge to reduce my sentence, stating my clean prison record, and my positive attitude. My sentence was reduced to time served, and I was allowed to leave prison six days after the appeal. I was put on two year's probation, so I couldn't mess up, unless I wanted a longer sentence.

My last day of prison was more of a going away party, than anything else. I received a good meal, courtesy of Mr. Lasado, and the other men affiliated with Tony wished me good luck. When I was released that next morning, I felt as if I had served ten years. The air smelled differently, the sky looked different than I remembered, and even the wardrobe I wore into prison felt differently on the way out.

Denise was there to meet me, and she brought my daughter Theresa with her. I couldn't stop shaking, as I ran to them. Hugging Denise first, and then stooping to embrace Theresa, I felt as if she knew me all along.

The photograph I had of her paled in comparison to my jubilant, innocent little girl. As we drove back to Denise's house, I closed my eyes, imagining the wonderful life that was within my reach.

CHAPTER 9
CHRIS PARKER

I received notice from Raymone that he was in the midst of creating a plan. He informed me that he would call me in a week or so. I focused my attention on Jacquelyn. Her main issue with me was that I did nothing for the community. She also had doubts about the validity of my drug busts. I had organized an event called Crime busters; a five-day convention focusing on the community building relationships with the police department.

The officers in my department didn't mind helping me on such short notice, since it was a positive idea, and I was an integral piece in the department's recent success. Setting up booths at the mall, passing out brochures, talking to citizens at organized meetings, speaking to public schools, and creating scholarship funds through fundraisers were focal points in our conventions.

I persuaded a friendly newspaper columnist affiliated with Jacquelyn's radio station to inform her about the events I had set up. He published articles about them in his weekly column. After each event, he called me back to provide an account of responses.

The first couple events, she didn't show up. She was critical of the police, and didn't believe the department cared about the community. I realized it would be necessary to take a more direct approach.

I called her show one night. The topic was, as usual, how to make a difference in the community. Jacquelyn was spouting off about the public officials corrupting the community.

"If they want to be helpful, they need to be honest," she said. "They need to reach out to the community.

I called in, stating only that my name was Chris from Milwaukee.

"Chris, what's on your mind?"

"Well, Jacquelyn, the police department seems to be trying to make a difference, and we all need to be supportive. That includes the police, as well as the citizens."

She replied, "Chris, the people would like to be supportive, but the people pay the salaries of the public servants, and the public servants need to go above and beyond their job descriptions. We all want the crime to end, but the decision makers and legislators are the ones who need to set the stage for the citizens' voices to be heard."

"There's only so much the police can do alone, Jacquelyn, but with the help of the citizens, a difference can be made. Criticizing won't get the job done. The department needs support. By the way, why haven't you been at the Crime busters events?"

Before she could answer, I asked, "Would you like to join me at the Crime buster's fundraiser?"

"Is this Detective Parker?"

"Yes."

Feeling she was put in a spot, she replied, I'll see you there."

Jacquelyn showed up at the fundraiser, meeting me at the ring toss.

"Well, I'm here," she said.

"Thanks for the support," I replied.

We walked to a booth where a small boy was throwing baseballs at three wooden bowling pins.

He asked, "I only have a dollar left, how man balls can I have?"

"The price is two dollars for three balls."

The boy's head drooped down, dejected. I jogged over to the booth, and put six dollars on the counter.

"Give it a try, son," I said.

The boy's first two throws weren't near the target.

"Come on honey, you can do it," said Jacquelyn.

I kneeled down near the boy.

"Think of it as a game of bowling. If you hit it between the second and third pin, all three should come down. I pointed to the spot I wanted him to aim at. Three more times, he threw the ball. Jacquelyn cheered him on. He came close to knocking the pins down, but he lacked enough strength.

"Sir, why don't you try?" he asked.

"I gave the balls to you, son. I'm sure you'll get it."

He looked up at me.

"If you do it first, then I'll know how to knock all the pins down."

"Come on Chris, you can do it," Jackie cheered. I grabbed the ball, took aim, and fired it toward the 'sweet spot'. The pins came crushing down.

"We have a winner," said the vender. "Pick your prize."

There were an assortment of large stuffed teddy bears, monkeys and ponies. The boy pointed to the large white teddy bear. As the vender handed the prize to him, Jackie clapped her hands. The boy showed her the teddy bear.

"It's beautiful," she said.

I could see here eyes light up from the simple toy. The boy smiled and handed her the bear.

"For me," she whispered.

"Yes ma'am."

Holding her dress, Jackie bent down and kissed the boy on the cheek. He giggled and skipped away from the booth.

"Wow, I hope your new boyfriend doesn't mind me escorting you around."

She grabbed my hand and pulled me close. I received a soft kiss on the cheek.

"Thank you Chris," she said.

We walked away from the booth with her head resting on my shoulder. Our time was spent talking about the neighborhood and what changes needed to be made. Jackie was amazing, intelligent and beautiful, with a good heart.

What began as an attempt to persuade her into saying favorable things about me became a genuine attempt to learn about making a difference.

This woman, who so quickly began turning the wheels in my heart, made me feel a change could actually be made. That was the first time in years I felt that way. We played games and joked around, as the fundraiser turned into a date. By the time Jackie and I were sharing cotton candy, I had forgotten about despising her earlier. I was really in to her, and by the way she held my hand, I could see that she felt the same. My relationships had been an album of blind dates and one night stands. Jackie felt unique. She felt right.

I took a vacation, for the first time in four years. We spent the next forty-eight hours together, from dusk to dawn. She was nothing like I'd ever experienced. We never, for a second, lacked things to talk about, and the match was perfect. The atmosphere was lovely, even though we barely touched. It was spiritual and emotional, allowing me to let my guard down.

She could see some of my impurities, as well as my fears. I shared with her my father's death, and the original reason I became an officer. She shared with me her plans for the future; her attempt to prove the media could be a positive force in the community, and her idea of true love. I was enlightened by her passion for doing the right thing, and it was contagious. In a lifetime spent with so much acceptance of being along, I was delighted our relationship was blossoming. My ethics were blossoming as well.

CHAPTER 9
JAMES JOHNSON

We arrived at Denise's house after a tiresome travel from the prison boondocks. Upon entering her house, I came to grips with the fact Denise had grown more than I. In actuality, I felt as if she had moved on from me. She had nice furniture, cleaned and polished, televisions, and stereos. The potpourri scents emitting from her vacuumed carpet gave it a homely feel.

There were baby photos hung on the walls; a clear statement to the time I'd missed in my daughter's life. They told a story of their own, one of a child growing up just fine without her father. It was a story I was unavailable to be a part of. I was partially filled with comfort, noting one of the older pictures of myself hung in a triangle formation with newer pictures of Denise and Theresa.

A conversation with my parole officer moved me to attempt to find employment. I didn't have much experience in any type of labor, with my towing job being a sham. I applied for a number of jobs, getting no response from most and no interviews from the rest. Possibly, my honesty about my criminal background hurt me, but more than that was my lack of real work experience. It was my own fault, though.

Avoiding Tony was important to me, knowing he had been informed, and was aware of my release. Tony had helped make prison less of a struggle than it could have been, but to turn my life around, I would have to stay away from him. He would only contribute to my temptation of wealth.

Four months had gone by since my release, and still I remained unemployed. Denise was growing uncomfortable supporting my child and me. I wanted to support her, but my past was a constant roadblock to taking my role as the provider.

With my criminal record, it was nearly impossible to find a decent paying job. Denise created a resume for me, but it could have been a blank sheet of paper as far as the employers were concerned. I grew frustrated with my own inadequacies. I decided to return to jail and speak with Preach.

As I waited for him to meet with me, a younger looking man arrived at my table.

"James, I hoped I wouldn't see you in here again, but it's good to see you."

I looked at his eyes, and found this man to be Preach. He was clean-shaven, looking much different than when we last met.

"Look at you, Preach. You're looking good, man. Are you planning on being in a prison GQ magazine or something?"

Preach softly laughed.

"How have you been?"

"You know me, I'm blessed as usual. I was given a retrial on my case, and it looks like I'll be out of here in a few months."

"That's great, man. Is that the reason for the new look?"

"Sort of. The Lord blessed me with a second chance. I thought I would be here for the rest of my life, but he allowed me to serve him outside of these gates. Praise the Lord."

"Halleluiah man, Halleluiah."

"So what brings you here to see me?"

"I need some help. I'm trying to change, but it's hard to change when you can't provide for your family."

Preach smiled.

"Just give yourself to the Lord, and he'll provide all things for you."

"You're right, man."

"Go to the Gas and Go station on Center Street. I'll tell them to provide you with a job. It probably won't be the greatest paying employment, but its church owned."

I thanked Preach for his help, and went to talk to the people at the full service gas station. It only paid four dollars an hour, plus tips. At least it was honest work.

On one rainy night, some of the drug dealers from a club I frequently visited drove into the station in three cars. They screeched their tires in the driveway, radios blasting, in glossy painted, chrome rimmed, and high priced vehicles.

"What's up with you, playboy," one shouted. "They got you down here, man?"

I remarked, "Yeah, just trying to make a little money, and stay out of trouble."

"I hear you man, stay up."

In his passenger seat was my ex-girlfriend Regina. Her expression alone ridiculed my employment. She smiled, and then leaned her head against his shoulder. As she twirled her gum in her finger, Regina was quick to show the diamonds wrapped around her wrist.

I felt like crawling in a hole, even though the young men didn't intentionally try to discourage me. Their material possessions reminded me of the lavish lifestyle I had known. Noticing an electronic bracelet on two of them reminded me of the trouble that lifestyle led to. I pumped their gas, received their money, and wished them a good night. I gave Denise three-fourths of my paycheck to help her take care of Theresa and the household. I didn't need much money, just a pack of cigarettes and a little spending money.

CHAPTER 10
CHRIS PARKER

I had known and worked with Raymone long enough to be aware of how he operated his shady endeavors. He was a perfectionist when it came to preparation, observing people's patterns, their routines, and their tendencies before setting any plans in motion. His motto was; men are predictable, and predictability is the right hand man of a killer.

I recognized his jackal like ways, a scoundrel who would surely seek to kill me once I put Tony away. It would be prudent for me to get him first.

Raymone, being a snake, refused to get his hands dirty. Two men handled his dirty work. Their names were Nicholas and Alexander. From first glance the two seemed to be average businessmen, brotherly in appearance. Nicholas had slightly darker hair, but they lacked any other distinguishable physical characteristics.

Their persona gave the so-called 'enforcers' a most sinister identity. They were able to kill an entire family at home eating breakfast, and walk across the street to share a cup of coffee at the diner, while reading the dead father's morning paper. Never smiling or frowning, they possessed a blanked stare, which combined with their eerily professional attitudes.

I was aware of the enforcers being keys to Raymone's plans, and needed to keep track of these Norwegians.

Tony had employed a new runner, and though I had no idea who they were, I knew the runner would be a target in finding information about his use of the enforcers. A rookie officer was assigned to me named John McCall. He was sent to provide much needed help with my investigation.

It would be too obvious if someone noticed me following Raymone's men. The rookie's operatives were to follow the enforcers and inform me whenever both of them drove together. I knew that would be a sign of their active involvement in Raymone's business.

I received a call from the rookie cop. He told me the enforcers were together, and headed to the inner city. I joined the trailing of the Norwegians, intersecting the pathway as inconspicuous as possible. Their car slowed down, their lights were turned off, and they stopped in the back of a brick house on Locust Street.

They wore dark gloves and black overcoats. Considering it was only drizzling, and not excessively cold, that was odd. The enforcers easily marched through the back gate, entering the house without any indication of a key being used, or any window being broken. The heater in my squad car wasn't working properly. I slammed my hand against it, but it had no effect on the unit. I could barely see anything in the car, so I decided to investigate outside the vehicle. The spunky rookie wanted to help with the investigation, but after an untimely argument, I convinced him to remain in the car and await my instructions.

Unable to see through the drizzle and thick fog, I temporarily lost sight of the men. I proceeded down the same path as the enforcers. I peered through a window, wiping the bottom portion of the glass to get a clear view.

I saw an eerie sight, one of the enforcers beating a young black woman who was tied to a cast iron heater. I was horrified and stunned by the force of the punches being thrown at her, unable to fight back. I kept hearing her scream, "I don't know, I don't know anything," getting bludgeoned each time she spoke. I was physically unable to move, as I watched this attractive woman's appearance changing with each punishing blow they took turns inflicting.

I fought through my petrified state, after noticing Nicholas grab a ball pin hammer. I raced in, gun drawn, just as he was swinging the hammer at her head. Distracted by my entrance, the fatal blow merely glanced the side of her head, still enough to knock her unconscious. The other man reached for his gun, but before he could shoot, I fired a bullet into his groin. As he sprawled to the floor, I focused my attention on Nicholas.

With hands raised, he said, "I give up." I knew they were deadly killers, so I didn't trust his surrender. Using the butt of my firearm, I struck the enforcer in the throat. As he gasped for air, I roared, "How does it feel to you?"

Finally having a free moment, I called the rookie, commanding him to send for a backup squad and an ambulance. I handcuffed both men, although there was a possibility one didn't make it through the incident. Checking on the young woman, I noticed she was at least breathing, although it wasn't particularly well.

Through the blood and numerous swelled bruises, she looked familiar, very familiar. She looked incredibly familiar. Oh my God, it was James's sister Laena. How did she get caught up in this garbage? I kept her breathing with CPR for as long as it took the ambulance to come, and she was taken to the hospital.

Distraught from the encounter, and the results of it, I walked shell-shocked from Laena's home. I had to reach James and let him know. I had been thinking about him from time to time, hoping to get back together with him. I didn't want it to happen this way.

I left a message at his girlfriend Denise's house. I was disparagingly anxious he would call back. I heard he was out of jail. What a way to spend your first days out, with your sister fighting for her life. Being a detective, I was used to calling victim's families with bad news, but this was different. It was someone close to my best friend, and someone who was close to me.

My voice trembled when James called me back and asked me what was wrong. "Laena's been hurt real bad. You need to go see her now."

"Where's she at?"

"She's at Froedtert Hospital, but you need to get to there soon, she's in bad shape," I replied.

I was hesitant to go to the hospital, but I did anyway. I knew it would be difficult to see her in that condition again.

CHAPTER 10
JAMES JOHNSON

Everything seemed to be falling into place. I had a job, my freedom, and more importantly, two of the people I loved most were close to me. I felt nothing could tear me down if I stayed out of trouble.

My serenity was short lived, as I received a message from Chris to call immediately. I missed Chris's friendship, and held little animosity for his unwillingness to help me with a lawyer. I needed to grow up, and tough love is an answer for a stubborn soul.

Something felt wrong about this message. I called Chris back to see what he wanted.

"Chris, what's up with you?"

"Just hanging, man. There's a problem. Laena's been hurt real bad. She got caught up in some drama, and she's at the hospital."

Simultaneously grabbing Denise's car keys and walking out the door, I asked, "Where is she?"

"She's at Froedtert Hospital. I'll be there in a minute. I'm leaving right now."

By the time I arrived at the hospital, Chris was there, sitting outside Laena's room.

"Chris, I'm glad you're here, how is she?"

"I haven't seen her yet, but everyone has cleared out of her room, so maybe the nurses will let us go in."

I walked to the nurse's desk, asking to see Laena. She replied, "You can go in, but she's still unconscious and very weak. The aide watching over her will ask you to stay a short distance away from her. It's our policy.

I walked to the door, with Chris following me, expecting the worst. My expectations were met, as Laena lay in the bed, nearly motionless. Only the sounds of the numerous machines connected to her body, and the second hand ticking on the clock were audible over her faint breathing.

The ticks were like stakes being driven into me, time slowly killing my sister. It was six twenty-three. I listened intensely to see if she were breathing. She was still alive.

Her hand twitched every twenty or thirty seconds, her forearms were loaded with IV's, her neck was braced with foam and steel, and her face, oh her face. They must have battered my beautiful sister, but as long as she was breathing, she was still alive, and still beautiful.

I wanted to hold her tightly and take away the pain for her, but I couldn't do either one. I dropped to my knees and prayed to God that he would either numb her pain, or that, unconscious, she was unaware of it in her dreamlike state. I prayed that he would heal her, or receive her into heaven.

I cried silently and continuously, being comforted by Chris's hand on my shoulder. I watched, hopeful from the timely twitches of her hands. Suddenly the twitches stopped, my heart cracked, and Laena's soul left her body. The nurses, by routine, called the doctors in. They tried to revive her, but their attempts were futile. It was for the best. She didn't deserve the pain that she endured.

The time was six fifty-one, and Laena was dead. I left the room, empty inside, and emotionless.

CHAPTER 11
CHRIS PARKER

Laena's death put everything into perspective. Sometimes we don't reach the pinnacle of life before our deaths. I had spent so much time focusing on being successful, and neglected the people that should have mattered most. There was my poor mother, for one.

She didn't deserve her son deserting her in a time of need. It had been twelve years and counting, and I still hadn't spoken to her. Jackie's entrance into my life nudged me toward changing my lifestyle, but Laena's death and James's sorrow pushed me to act sooner. I called my mother to ask for her forgiveness.

"Mom, hello, this is Chris."

"Who is this?"

"It's your son, Chris."

"Chris, my son Chris? I've missed you, honey. I've been wishing the day would come when we could...talk...again."

Politely I said, "Mom, I'm sorry that I hurt you and lost touch with you. It's not your fault that dad died. I know that. I knew it before, and I shouldn't have treated you that way. I'm sorry."

Weights lifted off my shoulders, as my mother repeated, "Its ok honey, mommy still loves you."

I promised to see her soon, telling her that work would keep me busy a little while, but that I'd stay in touch with her. I needed the drama to calm down before I could rebuild my relationship with my mother.

I focused my attention on Jackie. She was worried about me, especially after finding out the details of my involvement in Laena's murder. When the reports surfaced that the Norwegian enforcer I shot died, she was afraid I would be killed. I tried my best to convince her that everything would be fine, but she was a sharp woman. She could tell when I was feeding her lines. She knew of drug deals and dealers, and was fully aware of Raymone, and the trail of death leading to anyone who crossed him.

Jackie cared for me, and wanted to protect me from harm. My ego wouldn't let me accept help from her. She made no acknowledgement of our relationship to the public.

I was convinced I could handle Raymone and his men. Still, I knew that killing one of the Norwegians and betraying him would bring his wrath against me. My setup plan was seriously flawed now. My case against the remaining enforcer was flawed, as I learned of my failure to read him his Miranda rights again. Should I have read him his rights before or after he killed Laena? He would surely inform Raymone, if he hadn't already done so.

There was no way I could bring down Raymone or Tony now. The fame I would have gained from the execution of my plan was growing less important each day. Since the murder, I chose to concentrate on my life, letting Tony and Raymone battle each other until one of them killed the other. I could care less about either of their lives.

CHAPTER 11
JAMES JOHNSON

I was in charge of making all the arrangements for Laena's funeral. Before I could put my sister's memory to rest, I had to find out exactly how she died.

Tony Lasado was looking for me, since I had been trying to avoid him. He held the answers to my questions concerning my sister's death. He had something to do with it, but I was unsure what the connection was. I called Tony, telling him I was interested in meeting with him.

"Mr. Johnson, I've been waiting to hear from you. I'll be expecting you within the hour."

I knew Tony was upset with me. He only referred to me as Mr. Johnson when he was angry.

I drove to his home and was escorted by two armed men to his yard.

"James, it's good to see you, "said Tony, hugging me tightly. He patted me on the back very hard in an obvious attempt to intimidate me.

"Why haven't you called me? I know you've been struggling, and I got some work for you."

"Mr. Lasado, I'm not interested in your work, and you promised not to keep my sister as a runner. Because of your stupid ass lies, she's dead. Why the hell didn't you let her go?"

Tony's face changed, his graying eyebrows raised, and he began gritting his teeth.

"You ungrateful little bastard. I ought to kill you right now for even thinking about disrespecting me. If it weren't for me, you would have been broke a long time ago. If it weren't for me, you would have been dead in prison. If it weren't for me, for my...patience, you'd be dead right now. So don't give me that bull about killing your sister. Raymone killed your sister. I told her that you wanted her out of the game, but she wanted to make money. She made money. Sometimes you get to spend it, and sometimes you die trying. You know the game. You played it for a while. So if you don't want matching graves, get out of my face."

I'd seen Tony enough to know he never made threats without following up on them. This was not the time to be a hero. I walked briskly from his house, and heard gun clips being loaded upon my exit.

I screeched away, promising to stay away from his home. That didn't mean I couldn't let the police handle him. I left an anonymous message for the police, giving them information about Tony's illegal enterprises. It was a small portion of revenge, but revenge nonetheless. I could have done more, but that would risk putting my family in further danger. Violence didn't affect Tony, but messing with his finances did. I left it in the police's hands.

After organizing the details concerning Laena's funeral, I spent time reflecting on my lost, distant relationship with my sister.

Sitting in front of the mirror, I wondered how life would have turned out if we all were a happy family. Maybe Laena and daddy would still be alive. Maybe mamma would be around. Maybe I wouldn't have gone through the drama I experienced.

There was no way to turn back the time. I would give away everything I possessed to have my father and my sister alive.

I prepared for my sister's funeral.

CHAPTER 12
CHRIS PARKER

There was no joy, no excitement, no posturing in front of the mirror on this rainy morning. It was the day I was to attend Laena's funeral.

I'd always hated funerals, especially since attending my father's funeral. The thought of putting on your best, darkest clothing to view a dead body disturbed me, since it was an aspect of my everyday police work. It was even more disturbing when it was someone you knew, or loved.

The day seemed so much colder than usual, I thought, as I left my home to pick up Jackie. As I arrive at her house, and she entered my car, questions began racing through my mind. How long would I live, being in this line of work? How important is my fame and fortune if I'm not around to share it with those I wished to impress? How could I risk being eternally separated from Jacquelyn?

She was the first person to care about me, not the façade I tried to create of myself. I decided I would request a different position when I returned to work. The detective work was glamorous, but it would surely kill me sooner or later.

There were other ways to make a difference, and other positions I could accept which would keep me involved in the community. My father would have wanted it that way. He believed helping the community was a key in living a comfortable life. I finally realized he was right.

We arrived at the funeral grounds, meeting James, Denise, and their daughter at the entrance. We embraced, saying little, yet knowledgeable of each other's feelings.

Sincerely, I stated to James, "Do you mind if I tag along with you to your church next Sunday?"

"Sure man, you know you're welcome."

A smile came to Jacquelyn's face.

There were more people at the funeral than either of us anticipated, as I glanced at the crowd. Laena's casket was covered with an emerald green cloth, and raised above the gravesite. The rain slowly turned to snow, as I watched the air grow colder and smoky breath come from saddened mouths.

I noticed two men, separated from the rest of the crowd, paying close attention to me. I thought nothing of it, until I saw the gleam of snow reflect off something. It was a gun in one of the men's hand. The other exposed a shotgun, previously hidden in his trench coat. This was the last possible place I expected an ambush.

I was in shock. 'Not here, not now,' I thought to myself. Unprepared, I fumbled, reaching for my gun. Right away I knew the ambush was courtesy of Raymone. Everyone in the crowd scattered, including Jacquelyn, unaware that I had stayed behind.

The first man pulled the trigger of his gun, firing a bullet, which entered my left shoulder. Panicking, I wildly emptied my firearm in their general direction. Many of the shots missed their mark, but at least one found its way to the side of his head. He shrieked, and dropped to the ground.

In the midst of one blink, I felt my chest explode from the blast of a shotgun. The force knocked me on my back, gasping. I could barely hear someone say, "The police are on their way." By the look on the face of the shooter, he heard their comment too.

He turned away, leaving his fallen partner behind. He was sure he had performed his duty by shooting me. I knew I was in bad shape, watching my blood turn the slushy snow around me cherry red.

I thought to myself, 'Am I dying?

I'm not sure. This pain is unbearable, unfathomable. Am I dying? I've never seen this much of my own blood before. Does this mean that I'm dying? I can't really breathe that well. Is that a sign? It can't be my time yet. Things are getting so much better now. I know what's important to me now. I'm ready to make a change.'

'Is this a revelation of what could happen if...only if...someday? Why can't I feel my legs? This is terrifying. I should be hearing sirens by now. Silence, except for my arrhythmic, slow paced heartbeat.

Touching my fingers to the large holes in my body, I can tell one goes all the way through. That's not good, not good at all. Where's that damn ambulance? Ok, here comes help. I see their lips moving, but I can't hear them, and that's not good. Not good at all.'

'Jackie is kneeling over me, holding my head up. I want to tell her not to cry, but the blood expending from my mouth consistently muddles my opportunities. I blink my eyes a multitude of times, hoping to prevent myself from blacking out. Now the pain is fading, how ironic.'

'I must be dying. Yes, I'm dying.

I stopped blinking to get a good look at Jackie. If she only knew I was falling in love with her. We would have been good together. I wish James could read my mind, so he could look after her.'

'One last breath should be enough for re-membrance of this earth. One chance to inhale the sweet aroma of promise, the fragrance of second chances, and the scent of fulfilled dreams.

One last exhale of promissory love, unattainable success, and redundant almosts.

Ah, there it is. There's total darkness around me. The people are gone. I am gone.

CHAPTER 12
JAMES JOHNSON

I t was odd, dressing for my sister's funeral in the same attire I purchased with the money that helped kill her. I felt partially responsible for her death, knowing it was my influence that persuaded her to take the same illegal road I took. I wish I had a chance to share some of the negative consequences with her, ones that convinced me to change my ways. I missed my opportunity.

The funeral was arranged to be short. Due to the lack of money and bad weather, nothing extravagant was planned. Pastor Lattimore was chosen to say a few words before the burial.

Denise, being a friend of Laena's, came along with me for support. She brought Theresa along with her. Chris and his girlfriend arrived, which further comforted me. He even promised to attend my church with me. It wasn't the event or moment I had hoped to re-unite with Chris, but at least we had time to renew our friendship.

As everyone gathered around the casket, Denise and I left to inform the pastor of our readiness to begin the burial. While walking to the pastor, I heard a 'pop'. Unsure of what I heard, I listened closer. Another series of 'pops' were heard. I was sure the noises were gunshots, at the graveyard of all places.

More upset than afraid, I ran back toward the burial site, with Denise screaming, "Don't go back there James."

I heard another sound, 'boom', and it sent chills through me. Running forward, I noticed the crowd running in the opposite direction, towards me. Coming into view, I witnessed a man dressed in a dark trench coat, standing over Chris with a shotgun in his hand.

Chris seemed to still be alive, so I knew the man would shoot him again. I called out, "The police are on the way."

The man in the trench coat walked away, calmly stepping over some other man's lifeless body.

My best friend lay in the snow, crumpled in a bloody pile. I ran to him, meeting him before any of the others arrived. He was gasping, choking on his own blood, and struggling for his life. I screamed, "Call for help, somebody, just don't stand there."

A few people left, but most of them looked sadly at Chris. His girlfriend came toward me, asking how she could help out.

"Just keep his head raised," I said.

She complied, holding his head in her lap.

Chris lay on the ground, reaching for the wounds on his body. I took his palms and pressed them against the hold, hoping to stop the bleeding.

"It's not working," I screamed.

At that time, I could faintly hear sirens, but they were far away. Tears fell from Chris's girlfriend's eyes.

I just wanted someone to reassure me Chris would be all right. He was a brother to me, and he couldn't die yet. He just shouldn't die yet. By the time the ambulance arrived, Chris was taking his final breaths.

He looked toward his girlfriend, trying to raise his hand to reach her, but he never made contact. Chris was dead. The ambulance crew arrived, worked on him, and raced to the hospital. It was a formality, because they knew he hadn't survived.

A horrible memory added to a sad occasion, and my daughter was there to see it. I only prayed her mind was still tender enough not to have these memories impaled into it. We'd all suffered too much.

The shooter was a far off object now, but still within running distance. I plucked Chris's gun out of the snow, and checked his clip for ammunition. One bullet remained, good enough if I shot him at point blank range. I reloaded the clip and started my sprint toward the distant figure.

As I began to run, I heard Theresa scream, "No daddy, no!"

Looking at her, I saw her cold little face, tears barely able to stay warm enough to run down her cheeks. This was my last chance at freedom. If I caught the shooter and killed him, I might as well have shot myself.

There was no way I could live without my loved ones again. I'd be back in prison, for sure. If I didn't kill the man, I knew he would walk off into the sunset. Theresa stood on her toes, stretching to reach for the gun. She tugged at my wrist, gingerly pulling it down. There had been enough death this day.

I dropped the gun, watching the snow start to slowly bury it. As fast as I was running to avenge Chris, I moved faster toward Theresa. I held her close, allowing the rage to pass. I felt fortunate because I was still alive. The snow began to subside.

CHAPTER 13
JAMES JOHNSON

I t's been eight months since Chris passed away, and the snow had moved on. It took away the frigid atmosphere of death and replaced it with the warmth of life.

Much has changed in this short time. Denise and I got engaged; something we both knew was only a matter of time. I began attending night school, working hard to provide my daughter with the best possible home.

More importantly, I began my ministry, working on becoming a pastor. With the issues I'd faced in my life, I knew that I could be a testimony to someone facing the same temptations.

Today would be my first time giving a sermon. I was proud, standing in front of the church's mirror. I was also humbled that I, someone who had done so much wrong, would have this opportunity. The sun shined through the colorful glass window, providing a glowing inspiration, as I approached the altar.

Standing in front of the congregation, I began to speak.

"This is the day The Lord has made. Let us rejoice and be glad in it. Halleluiah."

The congregation responded, "Halleluiah."

"I'm so grateful to be able to see this day. God is good all the time."

"And all the time, God is good."

"I like to speak from Isaiah, chapter 41, verse 9. If you have it, say Amen."

"Amen."

"I took you from the far ends of the earth; from its farthest corners I called you. I said, 'You are my servant'; I have chosen you and have not rejected you. So do not fear, for I am with you. Do not be dismayed, for I am your God. I will strengthen you and help you; I will uphold you with my righteous hand."

May God add a blessing to the reading, the hearing, and the doing of his word. Amen?"

"Amen," said the congregation.

"Today, I'd like to talk to you about fear. There are so many things we fear; arachnophobia, the fear of spiders, acrophobia, the fear of heights, claustrophobia, the fear of being closed in. Name the fear you may or may not want to claim. All these fears have something in common. They are all fears of the world, created by the world, and they keep man magnetized to the world. The Lord tells man not to fear. Fear is not a heavenly thing; it's an earthly virus that prevents us from doing the clear and untainted will of God. How can we speak to the fear of rejection, when the word says 'I have not rejected you.' When The Lord is on your side, there is no phobia. He created all things; therefore, there is no reason to fear anything The Lord has made. I'm not saying you should go out and pet scorpions, or cuddle cobras. There's a difference between lacking fear and embracing stupidity. I'm saying that Jesus died for the remission of our sins, and promised us life and life more abundantly, not just in this world, but the world to come."

"My fear was the fear of change, but I no longer know fear. I know that if my life was to end, at least I made amends with my creator. I pray that anyone here would lose that fear infesting their hearts, so they can be whatever God has called them to be."

As I paused for a moment, the congregation began to applaud. I glanced through the pews, my eyes catching the most beautiful picture I'd seen since my prison release. It was lovely Denise, dressed in her Sunday best, sitting with Theresa on her lap. They sat in the front row. Behind them sat Jacquelyn, visiting the church for the first time. We had all grown closer since Chris's death.

"If there's anyone out there who would like to take the first step toward rebuilding their relationship with The Lord, come to the altar."

The congregation was hesitant, waiting to see who would be the first individual to approach the altar. Dropping to my knees, I cried out to the heavens.

"Lord, I have sinned. I beg for your mercy and your forgiveness. I repent for everything I've done that failed to glorify you. You are wonderful, amazing, powerful, and worthy. I love you with every sense of my being, and thank you for each and every blessing you bestowed upon me."

While I was speaking, members of the congregation slowly crept toward the altar. One by one, they knelt down on all sides of me. The number of people at the altar far exceeded those who chose to remain in their seat.

"Thank you Lord," I muttered.

I felt a sense of comfort flow through me. It was as if all the evil things I'd done were no longer held against me. Shards of shattered lives were finally mending.

I took another long, deep breath.

Looking toward the congregation, every person in the church was crying or joyfully clapping their hands. The lone exception was a man in a black suit seated near the exit of the sanctuary.

"Is there anyone else who would like to come to the altar?"

The man in black looked around, and began a slow walk down the aisle. I began to clap my hands as he approached. A chilling wind blew through the sanctuary, as he stopped in the middle of the aisle. He reached into his black suit jacket and pulled out a silver berretta. He pointed the gun at me. The congregation frantically screamed.

"Jesus, Jesus," I whispered.

He pulled the trigger.

'Pop, pop, pop.'

I felt an easiness come over me.

"Jesus."

Printed in the United States
31162LVS00002B/619-636

9 781589 394322